Circus Fun!

Elizabeth Dale

Illustrated by
Vicki Gausden

Reading Ladder

EGMONT

We bring stories to life

Book Band: Orange

First published in Great Britain 2014
This Reading Ladder edition published 2016
by Egmont UK Limited
The Yellow Building, 1 Nicholas Road, London W11 4AN
Text copyright © Elizabeth Dale 2014
Illustrations copyright © Vicki Gausden 2014
The author and illustrator have asserted their moral rights
ISBN 978 1 4052 8232 1
www.egmont.co.uk
A CIP catalogue record for this title is available from the British Library.
Printed in Singapore
57029/3

Series consultant: Nikki Gamble

MIX
Paper
FSC   FSC® C018306

Coco Joins the Circus

Coco the Tightrope Walker

Coco the Clown

For my grandson, Leo,
who's always a bundle of fun!

E. D.

For Egg

V. G.

Coco
Joins the Circus

TICKETS

6

Coco was thrilled when he saw the
tents. He had always wanted to be
in the circus.

Can I join?

'We need someone to ride a unicycle,'

said the Ringmaster. 'Can you do that?'

'Of course!' said Coco.

Coco was so excited. He didn't know what a unicycle was. But he wasn't going to say that!

Maybe it was a unicorn on wheels?

'Here you go!' said the Ringmaster.

Coco gasped. The bike had only

one wheel!

How could he balance on that?!

Coco sat on the bike.

He put his feet on the pedals

and wibbled . . . and wobbled.

Suddenly someone gave him a push.

Coco pedalled really fast. He was

cycling! Yippee! This was fun!

Coco followed the others into
the ring. The crowd clapped.

Just do what
Maria does!

Coco stuck out one leg, just like
Maria.

Then Maria put one foot on her
saddle. Coco did, too . . .

Then Maria stood up.

Coco was scared, but he stood up, too.

He wibbled . . .

. . . and wobbled . . .

. . . and fell off.

The crowd laughed.

They thought he meant to fall.

Everyone clapped, so Coco bowed and smiled.

Why are they all clapping?

Coco
the Tightrope Walker

Coco knew he was useless at the
unicycle. But he loved the circus.
'Can I stay?' he begged.

Okay . . .
I have the
perfect job
for you!

Coco didn't like his new job very much. He really wanted to make people smile.

So he sang as he worked.

Crowds flocked to hear him and buy

his candy floss.

Coco just couldn't keep up!

So he made his machine go faster.

The Ringmaster asked Coco to walk
along the rope on the grass.

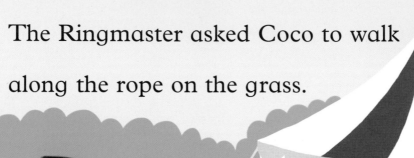

It was easy!

'Well done!' said the Ringmaster.

'You can walk the tightrope.'

Coco was so excited. He had a shiny

costume to wear.

He practised and practised.

Perfect!

At last it was time to go on!

The tightrope was so high.

Somehow walking up there felt

very different.

Coco wibbled . . .

Uh . . .
Oh!

and wobbled . . .

And then he fell.

Right on to the Ringmaster!

Sorry!

The crowd laughed and laughed.

Suddenly Coco saw Maria swinging very high. What if she fell?!

Coco ran to and fro, ready to catch her.

But he was too busy looking up . . .

. . . to see where he was going!

Sorry!

Coco knew he'd really done it this time.

He would have to go.

Coco began to leave the ring. But the
Ringmaster caught hold of Coco's arm
as the crowd laughed and cheered.

'You can't go,'
he told Coco.

'You're a star!'

Coco
the Clown

When the Ringmaster asked Coco to be a clown, just for that night, Coco jumped for joy.

'I've always wanted to be a clown!'

he cried. 'But I didn't think I was

funny enough.'

You are very funny – when you're not trying to be!

STARRING
Coco the
CLOWN!

They looked for a costume for Coco.

But nothing fitted.

Wear these to keep your trousers up.

The crowd cheered as Coco ran in.

But suddenly – SNAP!

Coco's trousers fell down.

As Coco bent to pick them up,

his hat fell off.

Archie stood in it by mistake.

Coco chased him.

Archie drove away in his car – fast.

Coco jumped on the back . . .

. . . and fell off!

Everyone laughed. Coco grinned.

This was fun!

Suddenly he saw the custard pies.

He picked one up . . .

Coco meant to miss Archie.

But he didn't!

As Archie chased him, Coco tripped

over his big boots . . .

. . . and Archie tripped over Coco.

Quickly, Coco squirted Archie with water from his big plastic flower.

But he got the crowd instead!

The crowd laughed and laughed.

Archie and Coco bowed . . .

. . . bumped bottoms . . .

. . . and fell over again!

The crowd cheered.

'Coco!' cried the Ringmaster.

'You're so funny! Will you be our clown

for good?'

Coco couldn't speak.

But his big smile gave everyone

his answer.

He was a clown at last!